Zahir Khan is seen as a co
realisation with a backgrou

Upon the instruction of his
study into other methods o. ... realisation. The result was
an understanding that all pointers to realisation are
essentially speaking of the same essence. This
understanding is liberating and has allowed Zahir to
convey the reminder in a way that is practical and
accessible in this day and age.

In this book, Zahir uses the medium of poetry to convey
different aspects of the seekers journey to realisation.
Sharing his story and insights in a down to earth manner
allows the reader to see that what is sought is already here.

Enlightenment in the midst of everyday ordinary living.

✹ *www.fallingintothemystery.com*

✹ *www.youtube.com/zahirtalks*

✹ *www.instagram.com/zahirtalks*

✹ *www.facebook.com/zahirkhanauthor*

Poems...

A man comes to a meeting, held by a teacher who he has waited over a decade to meet. He has seen the teacher grow and evolve, into what is in front of him now. He asks whether the teacher will ever collate his poetry so that others may enjoy it as he does. The teacher smiles; little does the man know that this comment has planted a seed.

Inspiring the teacher to present his poetry in the one place, and that like his prior work, "*Falling into the Mystery*" these verses might too make their way into the world. He decides to write about the moments that defined him and what transpired after he discovered who he truly was.

That teacher is me and the man who sowed the seed of inspiration is my friend, Stephen.

This book then is dedicated to you, Stephen. Maybe our meeting after all these years was to jointly present this gift to the world. Thank you...

Zahir Khan
November, 2019

Contents

Musings of a mad man in a "sane" world

They ask that I speak

They tell me others will listen

I have been shunned for so long

That I am no longer sure

Speak they say

People will listen they say

I sit quietly

With memories of days gone by

The ridicule still fresh in me

The wound still raw

I sigh

Words start to tumble forth

Welcome then friends

To the musings of a mad man in a "sane" world...

When I was young...

When I was young

I'd watch the stars

Wonder if they were watching me too

I would wonder

I would ponder

Was this then the beginning of my journey?

The Old Men

I sit amongst them

The old men

Dignified, honourable and strong

At the end of their lives

And yet they are here in another land

Still looking to give their families a better life

Discussing pensions and drinking tea

These old men

Why am I sat amongst them?

The Funeral...

My first memory is of meeting his wife

I am young and he is gone

I give her my condolences

And the smell of their house overwhelms me

A smell evoking my childhood

A smell evoking being home

Oh, how I wish I could return

To those days of innocence

They say he died in the masjid

In the month the holy book was revealed

After the Friday prayer

In his favourite masjid

Around the old men

Many come to see the one who was granted such an honourable death

I am at the graveyard now

Cold and damp

Lost in my grief

As my father approaches

I expect to be consoled

Yet he consoles another

Alone in my grief

I do not see the wisdom of it all...

In a moment...

In a moment he is gone

In a moment a life makes sense

As he smiles and extends his hand

I know my only task is not to break

With every sinew, with all my strength

I take his hand

He smiles

Timelessness arises

It is like watching a film

This doesn't seem to make sense

I become aware of every feature of his face.

That smile

Those lines

Those wrinkles

I am awake and yet unaware I am

A lifetime makes sense in an instant...

Zahir Khan. Reflections (Musings Of A Mad Man In A Sane World)

15

Broken...

She smells beautiful

And we are young

She is wearing that red blouse I so love

The perfume I adore

And that presence I worship

A life ahead of us

I will be happy for an eternity

And then she says it

I don't love you

A billion dreams destroyed in an instant

What am I to do now?

Blamed...

You should have known

You should have known

As the blame game starts

No accusation can be met with an answer

The destruction continues

The journey begins

And yet all I know is

Life is over

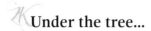Under the tree...

I am near her house yet far away

Memories flood my mind

That look

That caress

This love has become my nightmare

Thoughts swirl around

They will not stop

I need them to stop

I look at the bottle of sleeping pills

Soon it will be over...

You are stronger than this...

What do you do when your heroes disappoint you

What do you do when you realise they are as human as you

Cowards

Vulnerable

And weak

He stares at me and utters

You are stronger than this

The pills are working

I am staring at the house of God

As my body shuts down

And I feel the afternoon heat

I am bundled into a taxi to be taken to a hospital

I will survive

But something worse has happened today

A Hero has died in someone's eyes today...

The fake who was real...

Imagine an unsolvable puzzle

Why would someone create such a thing

Infuriating

Downright impossible

You were so right

And yet so wrong

Maybe you thought I'd understand your reality

In that then I can say thank you

You saw me worthy when many didn't

And yet I can't harbour the doubt

That you were the devil in disguise

A good one points you back to you

You certainly did that

I play just as you played

Consigned as you are to the winds of time

Imagine an unsolvable puzzle

I will never know your reality

And yet now I see

It was never about that

It was enough I saw my reality

It was enough I saw you...

Of this period I can say nothing more...

I'm falling into the mystery and I'm losing myself and yet even as I lose myself I find myself. What I really am and what I am capable of. It is a mass of emotions, feelings, thoughts and ideas, and yet finally after all these years it now all makes sense.

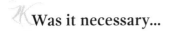Was it necessary...

Was it necessary that the word needed to pierce the silence and start the story of you, or was it all because you were a hidden treasure and wished to be known...

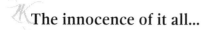## The innocence of it all...

I will never forget those days of innocence

The freshness of it all

The sun streaming through the huge windows

The world walking past

In this ancient place delivering a timeless message

What was said

No one knows

What was heard

No one knows

Sitting in the same seats

Week In

Week Out

A child becomes a man

And then the masters leave...

The Beloved...

Oh, most perfect beloved

Only you are

Why then do I sin?

To talk of two in love

This most grievous of sins

This most heinous and hateful of sins

Eliminate this sin

I am tired

I wish for there to be silence

With no one to ever know it...

This illusory Game...

I have fought myself so valiantly

Fought at every turn,

Oh, what a fool I was

Believing a reflection could defeat what was real...

In this futility I find myself,

And finally laugh like a madman.

I run from this lunacy called life.

I will not play this illusory game again.

Run, run to what is real,

Run into the arms of my beloved...

The only question now...

Everything triggers a memory of you

Excitedly waiting to return

Those moments of separation are so bittersweet

Those moments of union divine

Anticipation of annihilation prompts

The only question now

When will I go home?

When will we meet again?

Those who live in the heart never leave.
Promises are always kept...

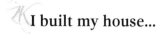I built my house...

I built my house

I built it strong

I knew it wasn't real

But I built it anyway

I had been seduced by that temptress called illusion

She told me this existence was real

How convincing her lie

How beautiful the tale she spun

How enticing the deception

I accumulated

I bought the lie

As it all came crashing down and her lies seen through

I saw the real...

I build now

I build

I build in what is real now

I build in what is true

And my building will last now

Last in what is true...

The Coward...

I have been a coward

I have not been true

I took the diamond that was given me

And hid it away from the world.

How could I have hidden a light that lives in every heart

How did I think I could escape

As I breathe now

I realise

This is the only song to sing now

This is the only thing to say...

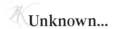Unknown...

How do you speak of that which cannot be spoken of

How do you remain true

This most delicious of conundrums

This most infuriating of challenges

There is just silence now

With words emanating as they do

Where do they come from

Where do they go

Does anybody know?

Can anyone tell me?

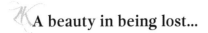A beauty in being lost...

So much has happened and yet it was just yesterday

When I held you and you held me

What happened of that time

What happened of those promises

I am an old man now

With memories of yesteryear

And yet no time has passed

Nothing ever happened

There is no tomorrow

There was no yesterday

No past, No present, No future

No coming, No going

No living, No dying

Such a beauty in being lost...

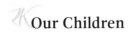Our Children

I remember that day

I remember that verse

I was a poet

I was a writer of verse

Now don't be silly

Grow up and get a real job

Let me kick your dreams out of you

Let me keep you "safe"

Years pass

I am that poet

I am that writer of verse

Life will always bring you home

Life will always get its work from you

Can the wisdom of life be surpassed?

I flow...

I write

I flow

I write

I flow

I write

I flow

I am only me

I cannot be separate from me

And yet I chose to feel I was

Like the dog chasing its tail

Knowing what is sought is itself

Knowing the futility of it all

But oh how we love our games

The game is gone

And in its place life

I write now

I flow now

No two now

Just one...

Zahir Khan. Reflections (Musings Of A Mad Man In A Sane World)

37

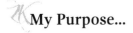# My Purpose...

My purpose now is me

My purpose is to meet myself

My purpose is to know myself

My purpose is only me

Only ever has been me

How could it be another

There are no others

The Treacherous Lover

Your glance is treacherous

Your embrace is treacherous

Your being in my life is treacherous

You charmed me with your honeyed words

You looked at me with such longing

You lured me in

And I gave you my world

And then you smiled...

You thief

You dirty rotten thief

You stole my heart

Treacherous one you took everything

And left me here with nothing

Screen...

Where does this go

Words appear on the screen

No rhyme, No reason

No purpose to it all

The best laid plans of mice and men

Demolished

Long gone

I sit here typing away

Words appearing on a screen...

Rest...

I am tired

But this will not let me rest

Still words keep appearing

Urging me to type

What is the point?

Boredom engulfs me

Has my inspiration left?

# Trusting...

To trust is to know that things will be alright in the end

To trust is to trust that which is beyond us

To trust is to trust that which is within us

To trust is to love

To have not seen, to have not known and yet to love

That is the true meaning of trust

To be...

To be grateful

To be thankful

To be abundant

To be aware

To be

The Funeral Prayer... (Djenaza)

Then pray my funeral prayer

For I am no more

Friends I am not here

I exist only as a thought

When that is gone

What is left?

The Glimpse...

The glimpse I could not accept

Was this really me

Is this my reality

The possibility is too much

As I retreat to my mind

I retreat to what is familiar

A thought remains

Is this who I really am?

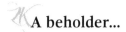A beholder...

They say beauty is in the eye of the beholder

But what if there is no beholder?

Or one to be beholden

Would that then not be love?

The elimination of the other

Would that then not be love?

The elimination of the other

That the lover and beloved are no more

That in this singularity

There is nothing to recognise itself

Can you not see that two in love is a sin?

That meeting...

When lover and beloved meet

Is it not a celebration

Is it not a day of joy

Beautify me

For I am to meet my beloved

Let at that moment

No trace of me remain

So I may truly honour my love

I am home now

Home in the arms of my beloved

A fool...

Let me sing my song

Let me drink my wine

I am not of you

I live in careless, reckless, drunken abandon

I no longer care about me

My reputation

My standing

What will could a slave have?

What of his desire?

Why complicate it?

Why be a fake fool?

Let it all go

Thoughts

Feelings

Emotions

Desires

The idiocy of knowing

And dance

And whirl

And live and love in extremes

For I am a fool

But what a fool I am

The Hostel...

I was a dream travelling

A dream seeking

And yet in all this drama

I was lovingly held

Until I realised why it had to be so

So much has changed...

So much has changed

And yet stayed the same

I travelled

While standing still

Searched

While being found

Found

And realised nothing had been lost

Changed

And yet was completely the same

A new day dawns now

And yet its been the same all along

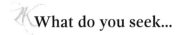What do you seek...

What do you seek that you are already not?

What has been lost that you tell me you are in pain?

Why do you say you do not know this and yet seek this?

Why play these games ?

What is your reason?

And now friend

Could you not put the reason down?

So I could cease and so could you

When there is no other

There is only this

Wouldn't that be wonderful?

Rumi..

The one who pointed to those magnificent ones

But was magnificent also himself

Stated

"If you are irritated by every rub, how will your mirror be polished"

There is wisdom for those who listen

For those who sit in the fire

For those who are irritated

And for those whose mirror is polished

Reflect the divine reality

It is the only work

Aashiq ka Janaaza Hai

Words fail me as silence engulfed me

What can I say that encapsulates the ocean

Knowing this futility what am I to do

All words are redundant

Destined to fail

Yet appearing redundantly

Yet serving a purpose

How do I go past this?

How do I sing this song?

Why is my throat constricted?

Why am I caged?

Why has the ocean chosen to be a drop?

What wisdom is there in the lunacy of separation?

What is that word that will bring solace to my heart?

And calm my yearning

As this agitation consumes me

As emotions rises

As ideas fail

Thoughts are calmed

Emotions pass

Feelings dissipate

The wave returns to the ocean

The 'me' is no more

Who could have witnessed this?

Who could even be aware of the silence?

Who could commit this sin of two?

And who is there to even know this?

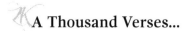

A Thousand Verses...

I could write a thousand verses

Tell you this

And tell you that

Regale you with stories of days gone by

How he flew

And she grew

How in ecstasy the dervish ripped his robes

How so much wine was drunk that no one stayed sober

Whirling to the early morning

Or should we talk about that beautiful discourse

That reduced grown men to tears

Or better still those parlour tricks

Golden Eggs appearing from nowhere

Letters magically materialising

Or even the fake who was real

The real one who appeared to be mad

But what is all this

Stories

Information

More material for the educated fool

I say leave it

Leave this too

Musings of a mad man in a sane world

Musings of a failure who only now is living

Is any of this any use to you?

Is any of this the truth?

Full of sound and fury

Wrote someone

In the end signifying nothing

I...

I represent it all

The whirling dervishes

The Sufi in ecstasy

The beggar

The mad man

The drunkard

The thief

The liar

The truthful

The holy man

The heretic

How could I be another?

There are no others

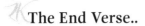**The End Verse..**

No one will ever know me And that will be my tragedy
And that will be my blessing